LUCKY O'LEPRECHAUN

LUCKY O'LEPRECHAUN

Written and Illustrated by
JANA DILLON

PELICAN PUBLISHING COMPANY
Gretna 2000

First printing, September 1998
Second printing, August 1999
Third printing, September 2000

*To Laura and Kevin Sullivan, Adam Esten and Richard and Lauren
Hansson, Julie and Amy Niemczura, Jaki Gerulskis,
and Antonia and Jaqueline Doherty*

Library of Congress Cataloging-in-Publication Data

Dillon, Jana.
    Lucky O'Leprechaun / by Jana Dillon.
       p. cm.
    Summary: On St. Patrick's Day eve, Meghan and Sean get help from
their three grandaunties and manage to capture a sly leprechaun.
    ISBN 1-56554-333-5 (hardcover : alk. paper)
    [1. Leprechauns—Fiction. 2. Great-aunts—Fiction. 3. Saint
Patricks's Day—Fiction.] I. Title.
PZ7.D5795Lu 1998
[E]—dc21
                                             98-18304
                                             CIP
                                             AC

Printed in Hong Kong

Published by Pelican Publishing Company, Inc.
1000 Burmaster Street, Gretna, Louisiana 70053

LUCKY O'LEPRECHAUN

Some people say you can't catch a leprechaun nowadays. Well, you can—but you've got to be smart about it. Those tricky little creatures will try to befuddle your eyes, twirl your thoughts, and outwit your plans every time.

On the eve of St. Patrick's Day, the O'Sullivan kids, Meghan and Sean, were sent to stay with the old grandaunties: Auntie Moira, Auntie Bridget, and Auntie Kathleen.

Sure'n you might think Meg and Sean would hate spending St. Patrick's Day weekend with three very old ladies. Oh, but that's upside-down thinking! All Meg and Sean had to say was "Pleeeeease?" and the dear aunties let them do whatever they wanted, just like that.

"Aunties," said Meg that day. "We want to catch a leprechaun."
"A leprechaun, is it!" cried Auntie Moira.
"One of those crabby little shoemakers?" asked Auntie Bridget.
"Leave Himself alone," said Auntie Kathleen.
"Who?" asked Sean.

"The leprechaun in the garden," said Auntie Kathleen.

"He's been there since we were little girls," admitted Auntie Moira.

"We named him Lucky O'Leprechaun," said Auntie Bridget.

"If we catch him," said Meg, "he'll grant us a wish!"

"And the stories he can tell us!" cried Sean. "True stories of long ago!"

"People usually ask for their pot of gold," said Auntie Moira. "But tricksters, they are. You catch one by holding him in your sight. Blink once and he's gone. Forget about it, kids."

"Oh, pleeeeeease?" begged Meg and Sean. "Pleeeeeease, Aunties?"

"Oh, all right, sweeties," said the aunties together. "You honey darlings!"

"What did we just agree to?" asked Auntie Kathleen.

They had to remind her, for of the three aunties, Kathleen had the poorest memory of the here and now, but as for the long gone, she could recall every detail. "Remember, Sisters? Lucky O'Leprechaun always lived under one thornbush or another. You'll need the shovels, kids."

Once outside, Sean said, "Okay, I'm ready. Where's the thorn-bush?"

Now that was a problem. The aunties' yard was surrounded on all three sides by thornbush hedges. Meg and Sean sighed and started digging.

At sunset Auntie Kathleen called, "Breakfast! I mean, dinner, darlings!"

As Meg and Sean, sore and dirty, went into the house, they heard a little snort of laughter. "Looks like you won't be capturing any leprechauns today," mocked a little Irish voice.

The kids turned back, but no one could be seen.

"Can we go out searching after dinner?" pleaded Meg as they ate.

"The day belongs to people," said Auntie Moira, "the night to the
Others."

"Pleeeeeease?" begged Meg and Sean together. "Pleeeease,
Aunties?"

"Oh, all right, lovies," said the aunties, smiling. "You sweet-
hearts!"

This time the kids used their brains, not their muscles. They slipped out the front door and tiptoed into the backyard. There, looking at the holes they had dug, was a wee man in green. He had his hands on his hips and he was muttering to himself.

"We see you, Mr. O'Leprechaun!" cried Meg.

The little fellow whirled around.

"Why, it's two wee children and sweet Auntie Bridget," said Himself. "How are you doing, Bridget, m'darling?"

The kids turned to see . . . no Auntie Bridget! They turned back.

"Gone!" cried Sean. "Tricked! I bet he's laughing at us!"

And indeed, they did hear snickering.

The kids trudged back to the house. Sean stood in the doorway and shouted over and over for Meg to come back out. But in truth, Meg wasn't there. She'd crept out the front door and into the backyard. And Sean, the rogue, knew it.

There was Lucky O'Leprechaun, how-are-ya, laughing as he listened to Sean.

"I see you, Mr. O'Leprechaun!" shouted Meg.

"You again!" cried Lucky O'Leprechaun, stamping his foot angrily.

Sean came running. "We'll let you go if you give—what, Meg? What do we want? His pot of gold? But is that really what we want? Quick, Meg, what?"

"I don't know!" wailed Meg. "I guess so! I guess the pot of gold."

"Granted," said Lucky O'Leprechaun easily. He took a candle from his pocket and lighted it. "I'll just put my candle down to mark the spot. See? And on my honor I won't move it while you get your shovels. Is that good enough?"

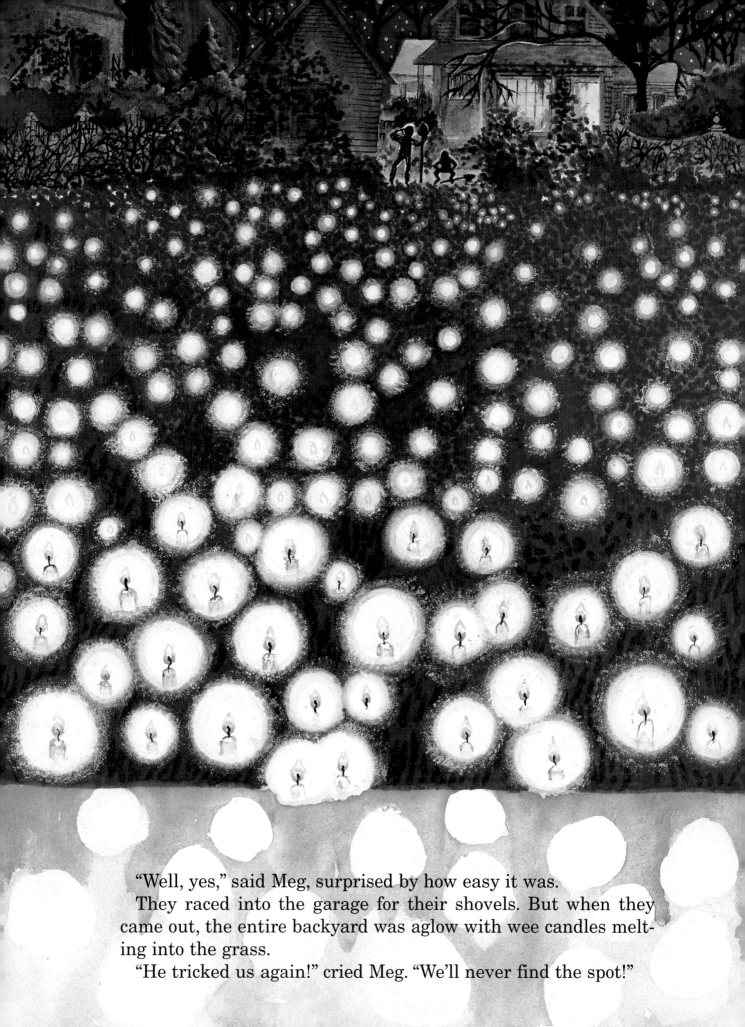

"Well, yes," said Meg, surprised by how easy it was.

They raced into the garage for their shovels. But when they came out, the entire backyard was aglow with wee candles melting into the grass.

"He tricked us again!" cried Meg. "We'll never find the spot!"

In the warm circle of light at the table, Meg and Sean joined the grandaunties for tea and Irish bread, the old dears' usual bed-time snack, you know.

"Sean and I have a plan to outwit that leprechaun," said Meg.

"How in heaven's name are you going to do that?" asked Auntie Moira.

"With your help, Aunties," said the kids. "Pleeease? Pleeeeeeeease?"

The trap to track the leprechaun to his home was set up as fine
as you please on the kitchen floor. Auntie Moira poured a drop of
tea in a wee doll's cup and placed a bit of Irish bread on a tiny
dish. Auntie Bridget let the kids put her old stepdancing shoes of
finest leather near the snack.

"And he being a cobbler!" she said, giggling. "How can he
resist?"

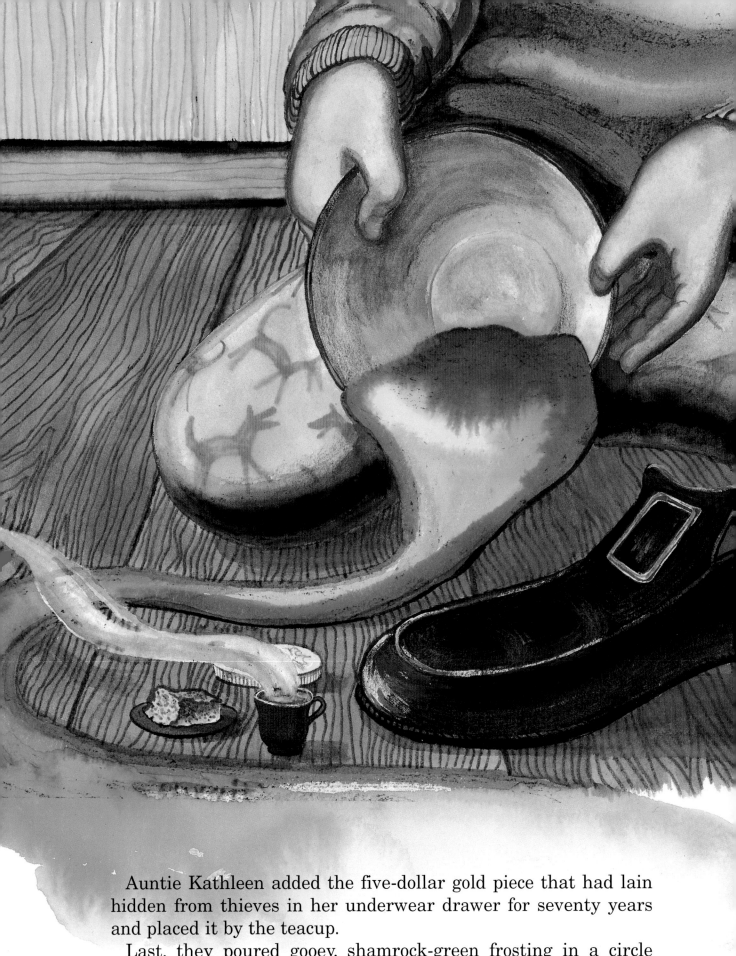

Auntie Kathleen added the five-dollar gold piece that had lain
hidden from thieves in her underwear drawer for seventy years
and placed it by the teacup.

Last, they poured gooey, shamrock-green frosting in a circle
around the trap.

St. Patrick's Day morn the kids leaped out of bed and raced downstairs.

Auntie Moira and Auntie Bridget were staring at the trap.

"It was Himself!" crowed Auntie Moira. "The little manny was here!"

Indeed, the gold coin was gone. The food was eaten.

"Glory be, the little divil cut a piece of leather from my shoe!" cried Auntie Bridget with delight.

"It worked!" shouted Sean. "Look! There are tiny frosting foot-prints leading to the back door. Come on, let's follow them!"

They opened the hall door to find Auntie Kathleen, on her hands and knees, scrubbing the floor.

"There was frosting all over the floor," she said, "but don't worry. I've cleaned it up, bright and shiny again."

"Musha! You didn't!" cried Auntie Moira.

But Meg and Sean ran past Auntie Kathleen and out the door. The green footprints began again and led to a hole in the ground under a thornbush.

"But how do we get him to come out?" whispered Sean.

Auntie Bridget removed one of her gold earrings. "Put it outside his door, dearies, and hide."

Sure'n it didn't take long before the little miser came out with his eyes aglow, staring at the gold.

"We see you, Lucky O'Leprechaun!" shouted Meg, pouncing on him.

"A fine how-do-you-do!" cried the little cobbler.

"Bring the wee fellow inside!" squealed Auntie Kathleen.

Lucky O'Leprechaun saw he was in a tight spot. "If it's all the same to you, my fine colleen Meg," he said in a voice laden with blarney, "I'm not interested in talking to anyone, including that sport Sean beside you or even that trinity of old girls, your aunties. So I'll be on my way, begging your pardon, so long, ta ta, see you some other time . . ."

Meg didn't answer. She marched into the house and placed him on the table.

"Ask for his pot of gold," warned Auntie Moira, "before he tricks you again."

"First we want to ask questions," said Sean. "Like, how old are you?"

"Nosey child," griped the shoemaker. "You're every bit as nosey as your great-great-grandfather Kevin, back in Ireland, who was always sneaking up on me and asking questions. But you're not half as bad as your relative Nosey-Nosey Deirdre, the one who married the Viking, back a thousand years ago."

"Did you know all our relatives then, all the way back?" asked Meg.

"Too well," snapped the leprechaun. "Enough said."

"How did you get to America?" asked Sean.

"Wouldn't you like to know," said the little man.

"Tell us about the Little People," said Meg.

"It's a long story and I haven't got time to chat," said Lucky O'Leprechaun stubbornly. "I'm not answering another nosey question."

Meg and Sean whispered into each other's ear and nodded.

"We have our wish," said Meg.

"Well?" demanded the leprechaun. He hugged Auntie Bridget's gold earring tightly to his chest. "Well, what is it?"

The aunties leaned forward to hear.

"Our wish," said Meg, "is that you come back to us every St. Patrick's Day and answer all our questions!"

"No gold?" asked the little miser, looking truly shocked.

"With gold we could only buy things that anyone can buy," said Meg. "It would soon be gone."

"But hardly anyone in the world has a leprechaun to talk to," said Sean.

"Agreed!" shouted Lucky O'Leprechaun happily. "I'll do it!"

"See you next year," called Meg as the leprechaun leaped off the table.

"On St. Patrick's Day!" Lucky O'Leprechaun shouted. "Top of the morning to you all!"

"And the rest of the day to yourself!" piped Sean, in true St. Paddy's Day style.